Topsy and Tim

AT THE ZOO

Jean and Gareth Adamson

BLACKIE: LONDON AND GLASGOW

Blackie & Son, Ltd., 5 Fitzhardinge Street, Portman Square, London, W.1.
Bishopbriggs, Glasgow
Blackie & Son (India) Ltd., Bombay.

216. 89015. 2

Topsy and Tim were going to the zoo. First they made sure that Wiggles the rabbit, Sam the goldfish and Kitty the cat had all they needed for their day at home.

"I wonder if any of the zoo animals would like to come and live with us?" said Tim on the bus.

"We could ask them," said Topsy.

"Animals can't answer questions!" said Tim.

Topsy and Tim met the penguins first at the zoo. They looked like funny old men as they waddled along. Then they dived into their pool and swam beautifully.

Topsy and Tim would have liked the penguins to come home with them, but the penguins looked very happy in the zoo.

There were a lot of parrots in the aviary, all making a dreadful noise.

Topsy had heard that parrots could answer questions, so she asked one:

"Would you like to come home with us?"

"Ripe bananas, brown bread," squawked the parrot.

"I'm afraid parrots don't give sensible answers," said Dad.

"Look at the elephant," shouted Tim. Topsy and Tim waited their turn with the other children. Soon they were swaying along on the elephant's back.

"We're the highest in the whole zoo," said Tim.

Then they saw a giraffe. She was higher still, although her feet were on the ground.

They ate their sandwiches on a bench. A hippopotamus watched them.

Dad asked a zoo-keeper if they could give the hippopotamus some sandwiches.

"Yes, if you know how," said the zoo-keeper.

The hippopotamus knew how. He opened his enormous mouth, and they tossed sandwiches in, one by one.

"You didn't ask the hippopotamus to come home with us—or the elephant," said Tim.

"They're too big," said Topsy. "They might tread on Kitty."

"Look!" said Tim. "Horses in football jerseys.

As though they had heard him, the zebras began to show how they could kick. One kicked the other with his back hooves. He was only being playful, but it looked a hard, painful kick.

"I don't think we could do with zebras at home," said Dad. "They might kick *us* by mistake."

The zoo had suddenly got busy. A lot of people were hurrying along the path. Some naughty schoolboys had run away from their teacher. They were getting in everybody's way.

Dad had to shout sternly, "Now, now! Stop pushing!"

Suddenly Mummy said, "Where's Tim?"

Topsy and Mummy couldn't see Tim anywhere. Dad ran along the path to look for him.

Poor Tim had been swept along by the crowd, all the way to the lions' cages. He told a lady he was lost, and she was very kind. But he *was* pleased to see Dad.

Bert
Lilly
LION
HOUSE

The zoo-keepers had brought huge lumps of meat for the lions. It was fun watching the lions enjoying their food. That was what everyone had been hurrying to see.

It was tea-time. The café was full.

Mummy found a slot-machine that sold tea in paper cups. It sold orange-drinks and chocolate too, but not bread and butter. Topsy and Tim thought it was a good slot-machine.

A giant tortoise was eating lettuce for tea.
"Would he come home with us?" asked Topsy.
"He'd take too long to get there," said Dad.

Topsy and Tim wanted to take all the monkeys home.

But it was time for Mummy and Dad to take Topsy and Tim home.

Mummy took them off the bus at the pet shop.

"Can you see any zoo animals here?" she asked.

There were kittens, puppies, hamsters, budgerigars . . . but Topsy and Tim had not seen these at the zoo.

Then Tim saw a tortoise. He was much smaller than the zoo's giant tortoise but he looked the same apart from that.

"Let's take the tortoise home with us," said Mummy.

Puppy
biscuits

Topsy and Tim called the tortoise 'Nosey' because he examined everything in the garden. Kitty and Wiggles seemed to like him. Topsy brought Sam, in his bowl, to meet Nosey.

"I don't know why we go to the zoo," said Dad. "We've got our own zoo at home."

Tiger

MORE ADVENTURES OF TOPSY AND TIM IN:

Topsy and Tim's **MONDAY BOOK**
Topsy and Tim's **TUESDAY BOOK**
Topsy and Tim's **WEDNESDAY BOOK**
Topsy and Tim's **THURSDAY BOOK**
Topsy and Tim's **FRIDAY BOOK**
Topsy and Tim's **SATURDAY BOOK**
Topsy and Tim's **SUNDAY BOOK**
Topsy and Tim's **FOGGY DAY**
Topsy and Tim **GO FISHING**
Topsy and Tim **AT THE FOOTBALL MATCH**
Topsy and Tim's **BONFIRE NIGHT**
Topsy and Tim's **SNOWY DAY**
Topsy and Tim **GO ON HOLIDAY**
Topsy and Tim **AT THE SEASIDE**
Topsy and Tim **AT SCHOOL**